Jonathan & Martha

Φ

Jonathan was lonely.
He lived on the left
side of the tree.

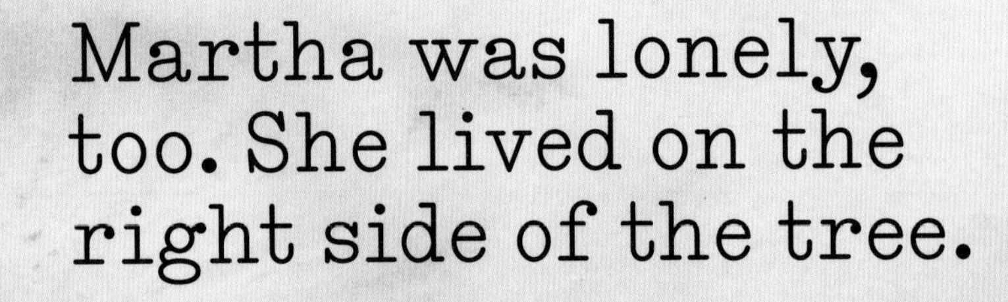

Martha was lonely, too. She lived on the right side of the tree.

One
day

a big,

juicy
pear

landed on the ground.

Jonathan wanted
to eat the pear.

Martha wanted to
eat the pear, too.

Jonathan nibbled
from the left.

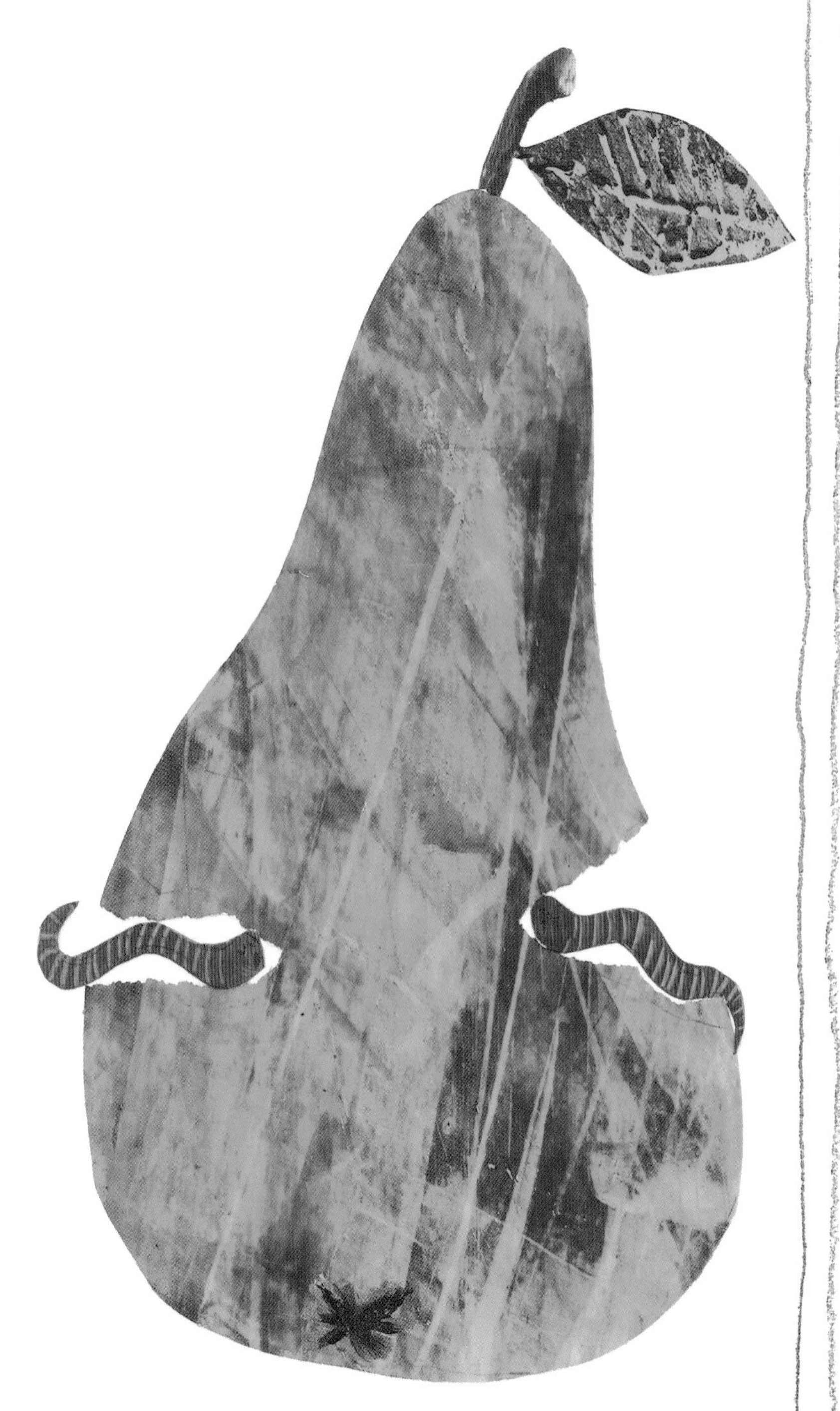

Martha nibbled
from the right.

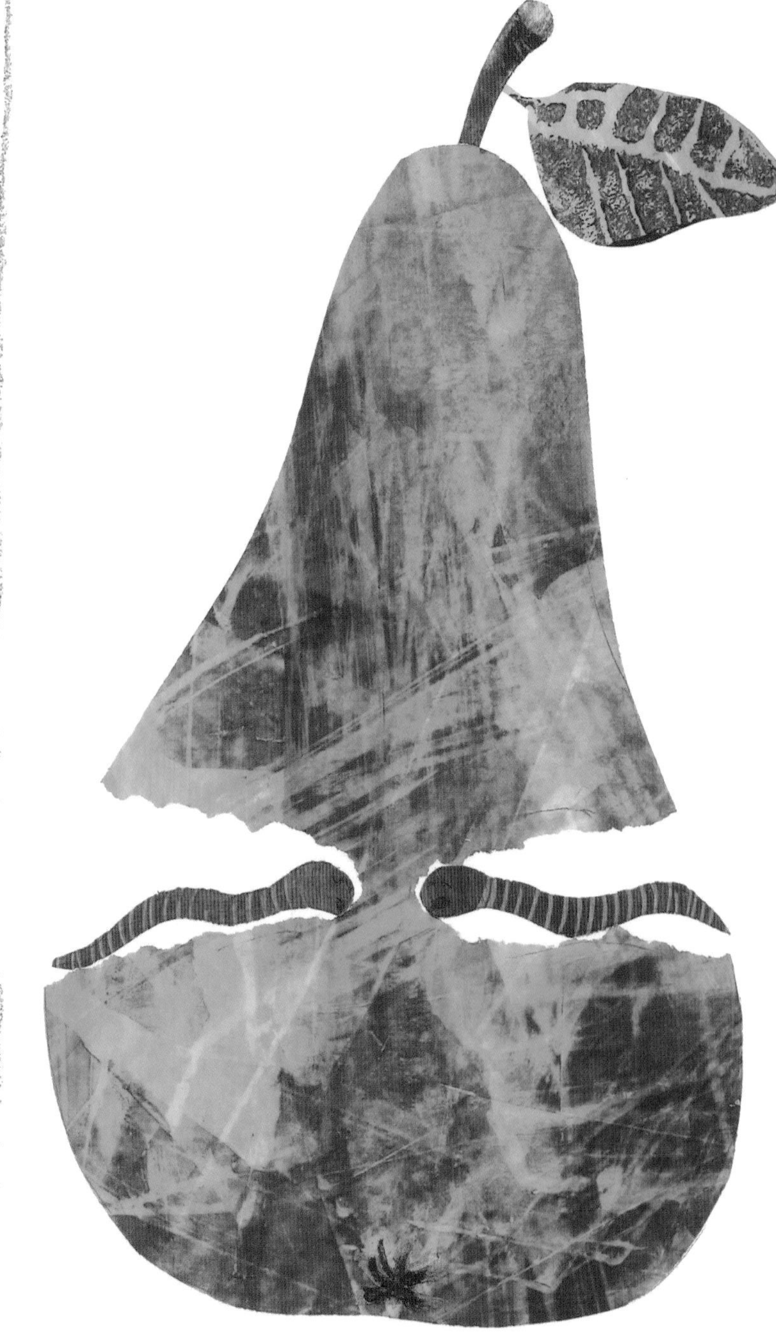

They nibbled and
they nibbled.

And this is how
they met!

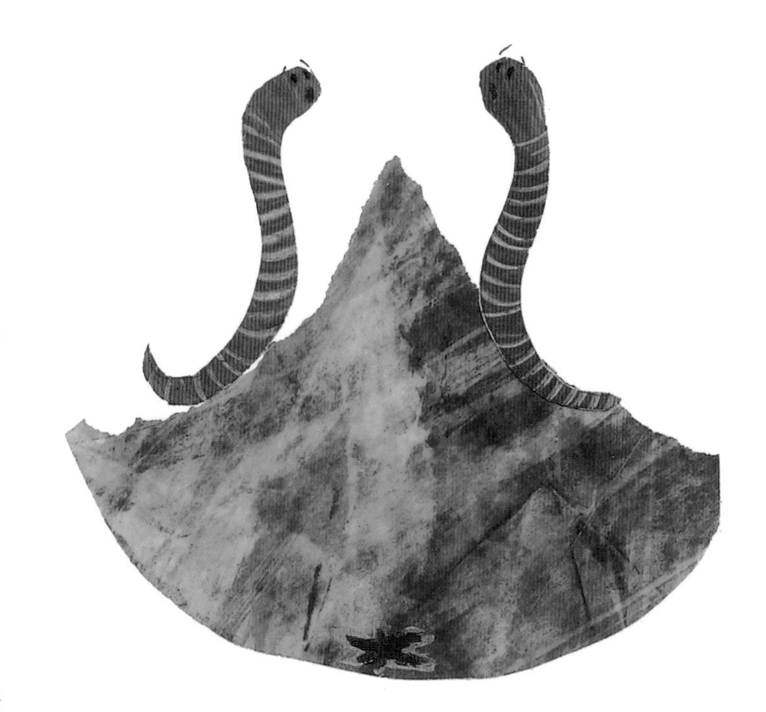

Jonathan wanted to fight.
Martha wanted to fight.

So they fought

and they tussled,

and tangled a bit
more, until...

they became one!

They had no other choice.
Jonathan and Martha had
to stay together...

and they had to share.

They shared big
things.

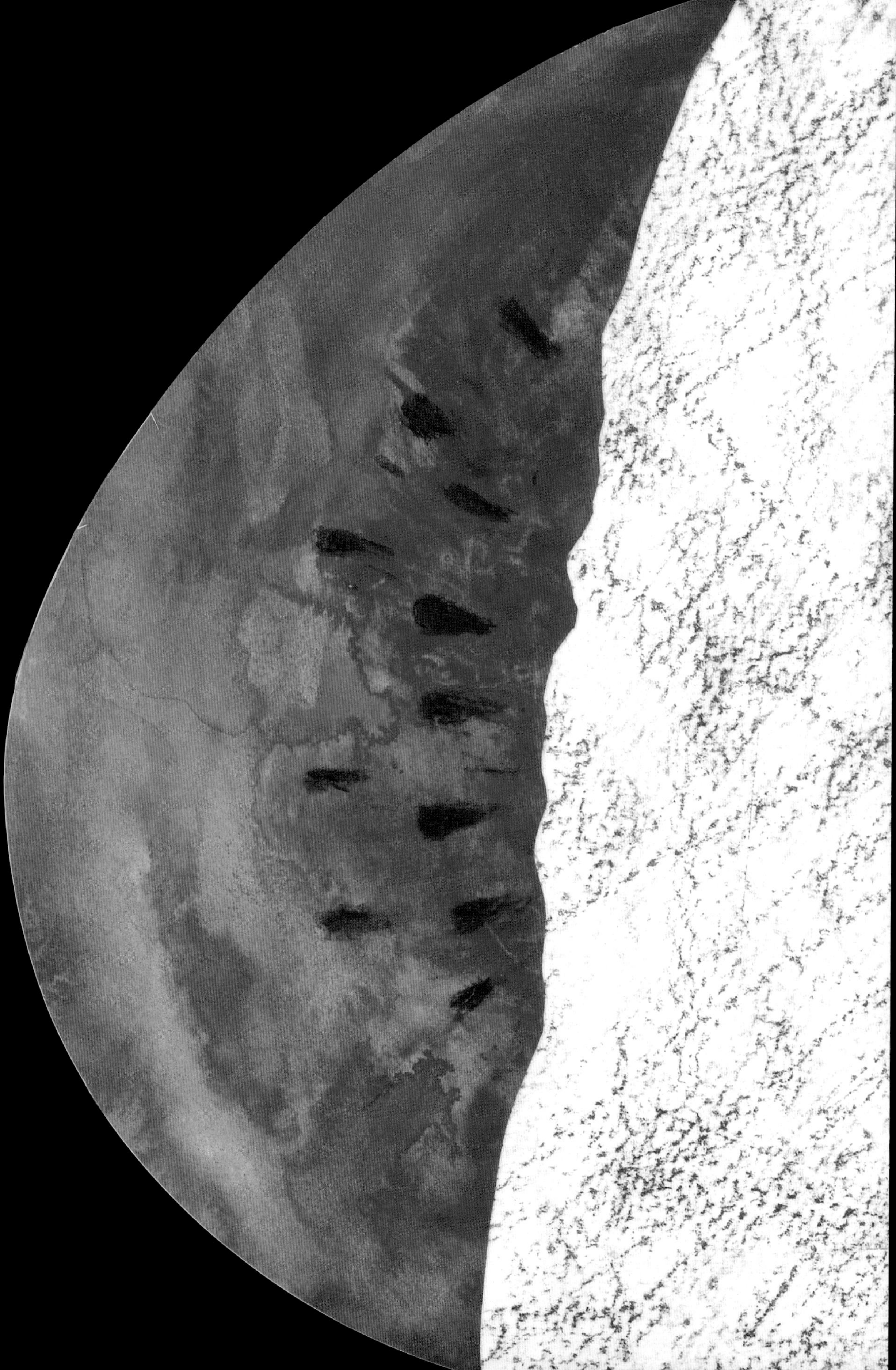

They shared small things, too.

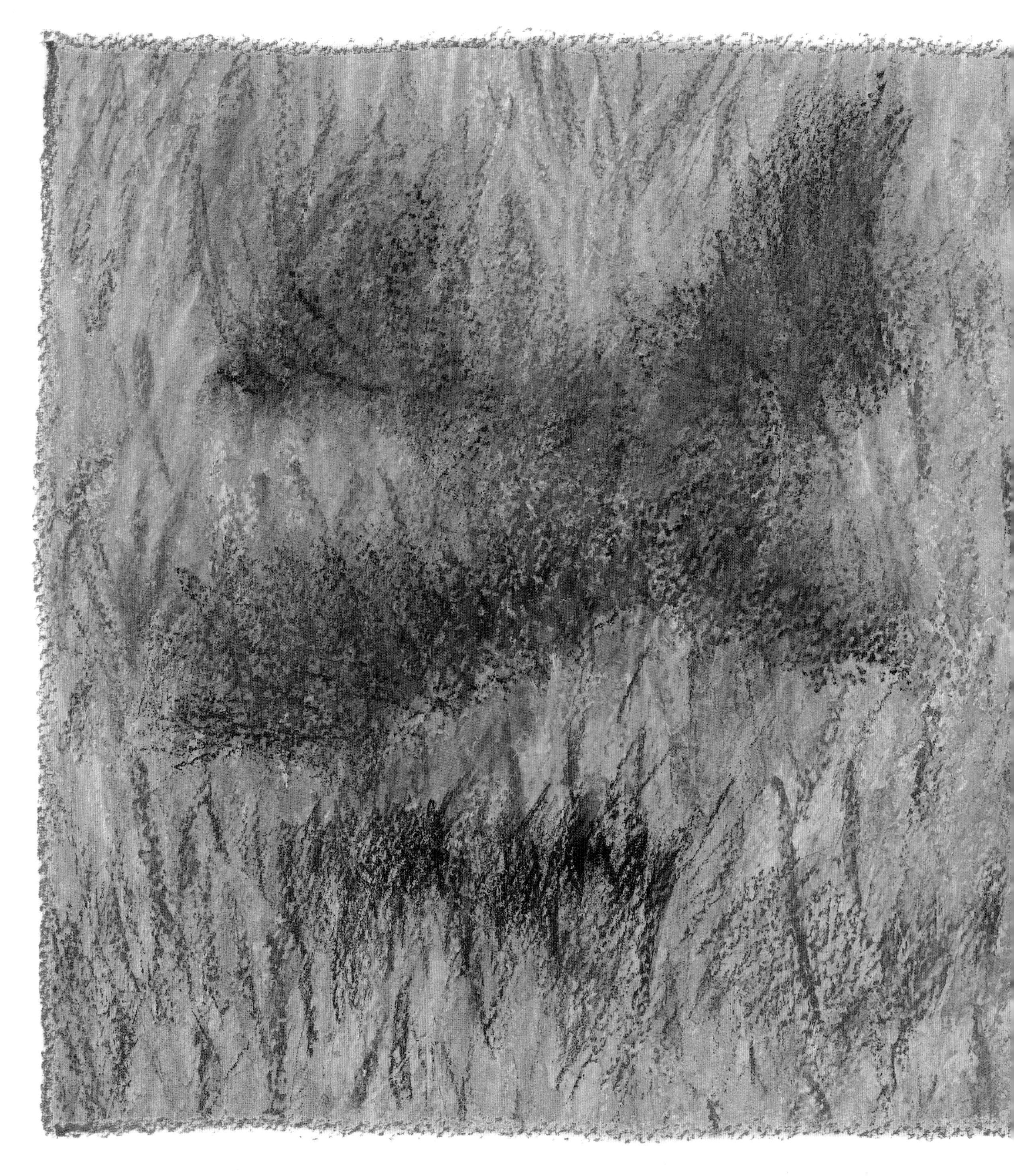

Sharing was
fun until...

a big hungry bird
flew into the garden.

He pecked off Jonathan's
and Martha's tails.

Ouch!

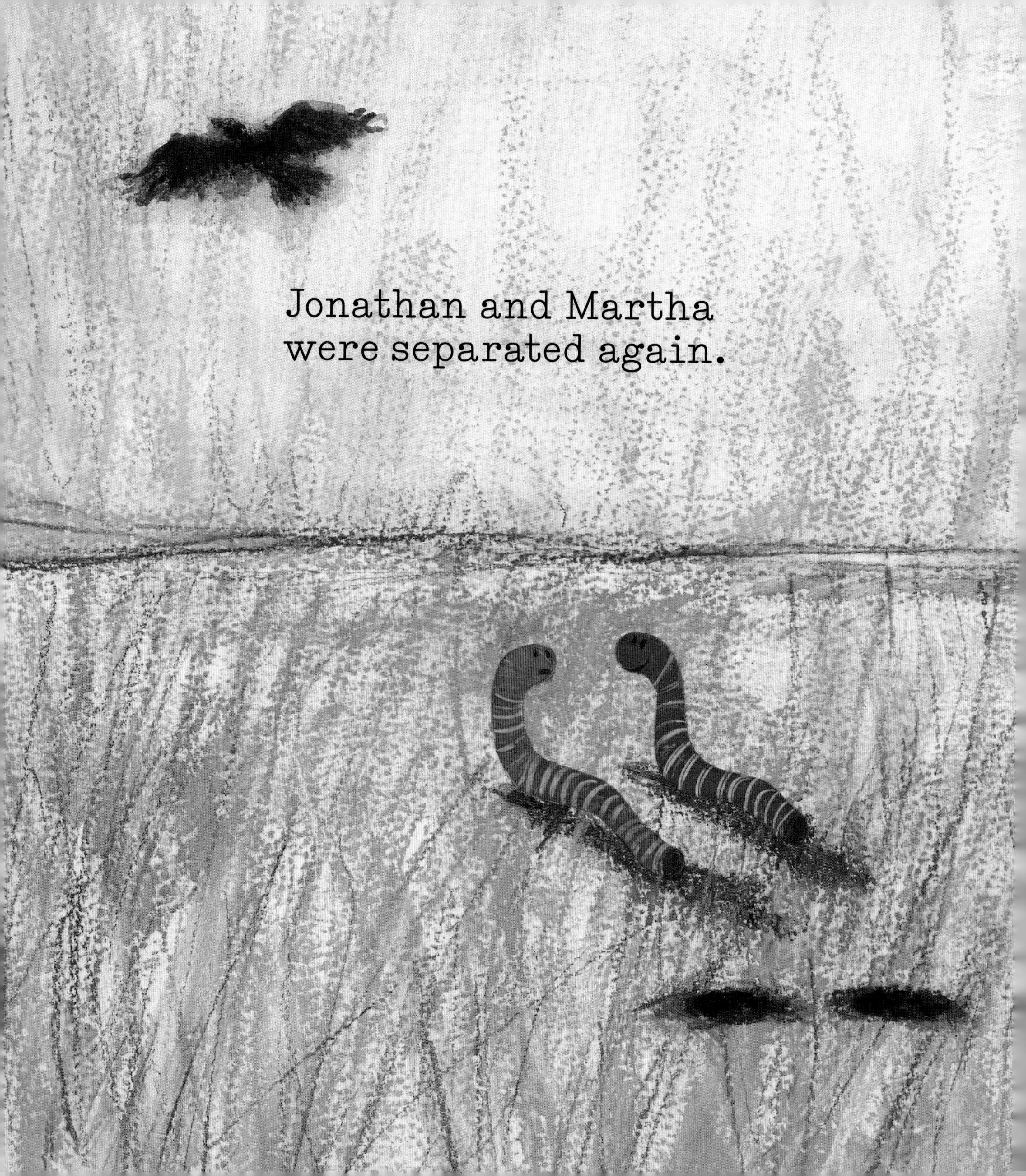

Jonathan and Martha
were separated again.

But now they *wanted* to stay together and they *wanted* to share.

They shared a
wedding cake...

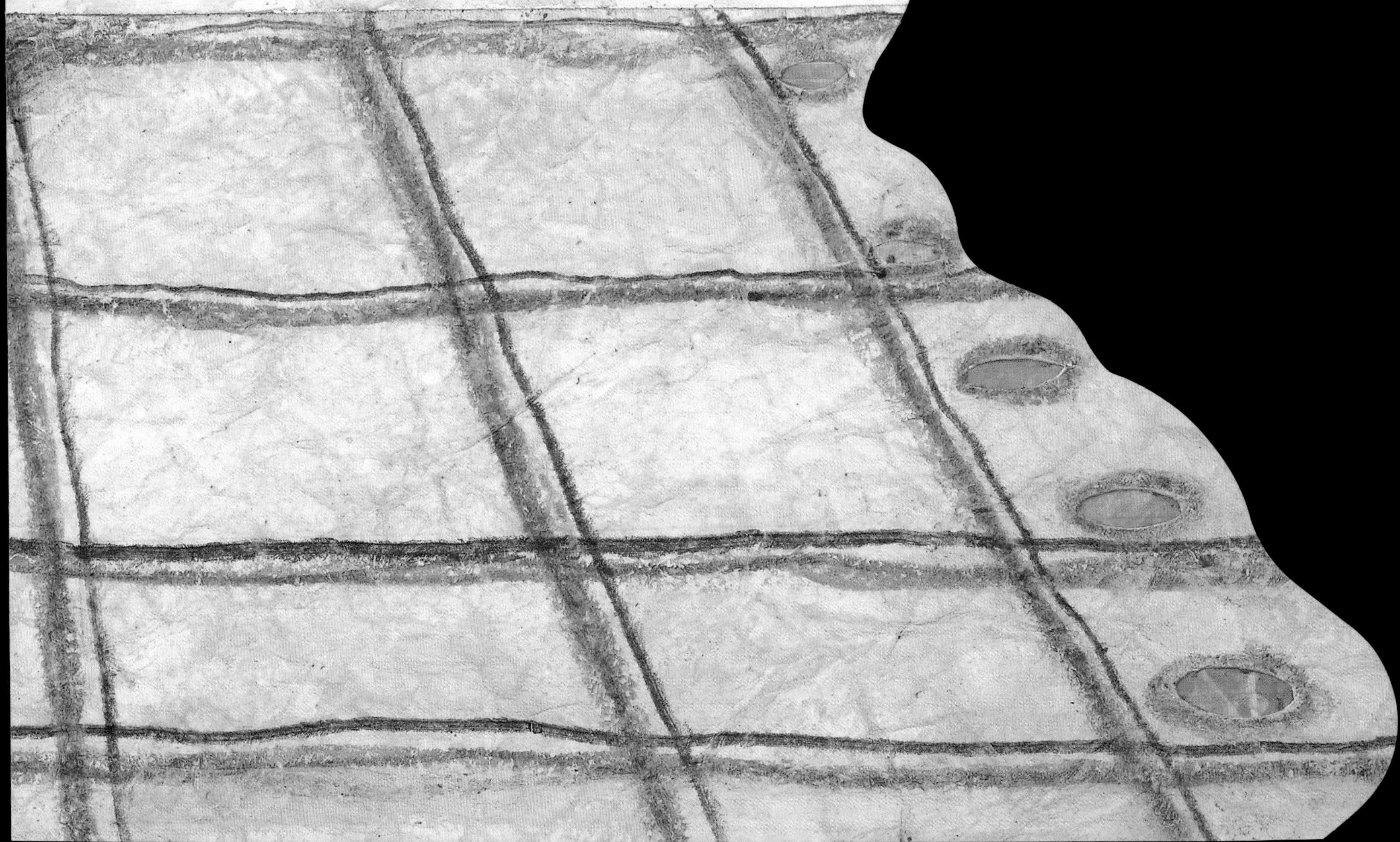

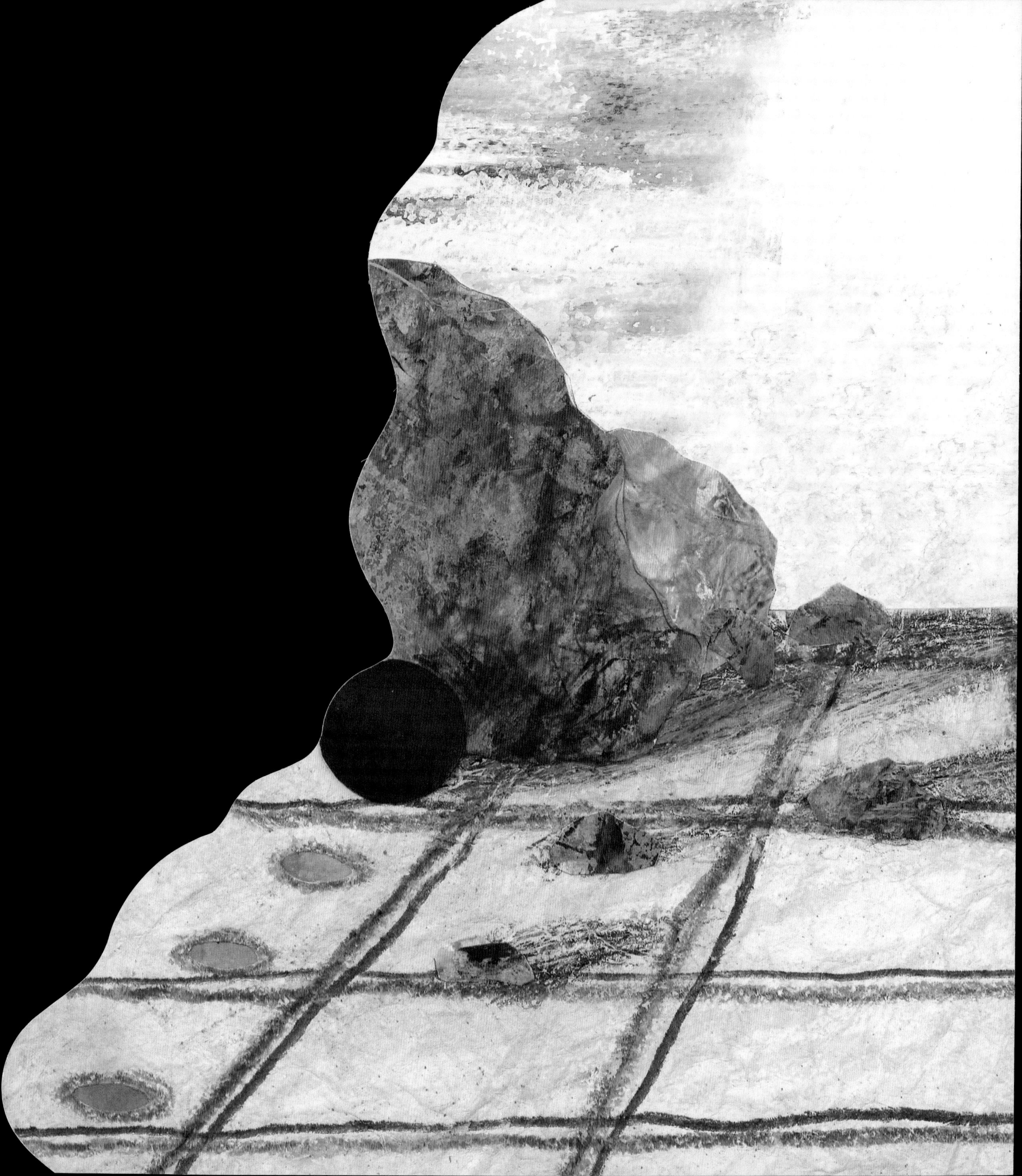

and they lived
happily ever after.

For Markéta

Phaidon Press Limited
Regent's Wharf
All Saints Street
London N1 9PA

Phaidon Press Inc.
180 Varick Street
New York, NY 10014

www.phaidon.com

ISBN 978 0 7148 6351 1
004-0112

A CIP catalogue record for this book
is available from the British Library.

Commissioning Editor: Rachel Williams
Production Controller: Anne Rennie
Jacket design by Hans Stofregen

Printed in China